MW01172255

Bringing Christmas Home

Other books by Leslie Anne Tarabella

THE MAJORETTES ARE BACK IN TOWN -
AND OTHER THINGS TO LOVE ABOUT THE
SOUTH

EXPLODING HUSHPUPPIES - MORE
STORIES FROM HOME

Visit leslieannetarabella.com

LESLIE ANNE TARABELLA

Bringing Christmas Home

A True Story

Liberty Blue Press

Cover design by: Robert Tarabella
Illustration by: Iana Zaalishvili

ISBN: 9798839667488 (Hardcover)

For
Harrison & Balto
and
Joseph & Snowy,

Friends forever.

People of all ages enjoy stories that remind them of their childhood toys. If you are a young reader, you may find this list of unfamiliar words and phrases helpful.

Darn socks - *to mend holes in socks with a needle and thread*
Knickerbocker - *Dutch descendant in New York*
Brogue - *an Irish accent*
Condolences - *an expression of sadness*
Pram - *a four-wheeled baby stroller*
Feigned - *pretended or disguised*
Crocheted doilies - *hand-sewn delicate lace*
Brusque - *Blunt or gruff*
Ominous - *threatening*
Diagnosis - *finding the cause of a problem*
Schoenau & Hoffmeister - *a German doll*
Boisterous - *jolly, noisy and rowdy*
Revelry - *festive celebration*
Reminisce - *remember past experience*

Did Mary and Joseph live in New York City?

This is a true Christmas story that begins with Mary and Joseph — but not the Mary and Joseph who traveled to Bethlehem and had a baby in a manger. This Mary and Joseph lived in New York City in the 1920s.

Joseph was the father, and Mary was his little girl. When Mary was four years old, her father gave her a Christmas gift she truly loved, but a devastating event destroyed it, leaving the little girl heartbroken.

Mary learned the love of a true friend lasts forever — and you never know what miracle you'll find at Christmas.

Rock and chat

"The final count was around 30,000, but that was only in the city. Thousands and thousands more died around the world."

Carlie looked shocked. "I've never even heard of the Spanish flu," she said. "How old were you when this happened?"

Mary continued to rock in the shade of the porch and said, "I was only two years old. It was 1918, and my parents and I lived in an apartment on a beautiful tree- lined street in New York."

Carlie arranged her clipboard on the side table and poured Mary a glass of lemonade. Her job at the senior living community allowed her to hear all kinds of stories, but this was something new to her. Some days her job was like reading a history book. Other days, it was more like a comic book, and a bad one at that — the kind that uses stale dad jokes. But overall, she loved hearing the older generation's stories.

Mary had only recently moved into the retirement community, so her stories were still new. She was reluctant to socialize, but Carlie had been so sweet, Mary couldn't refuse her invitation to attend the "rock and chat" on the shared porch.

The ceiling fan slowly rotated with a squeak while Mary waited for the others to arrive.

About that time, Horace walked over from his cottage with the help of a cane and plopped down on the rocking chair next to Mary. "How-de-do," he said.
"Good afternoon, yourself," replied the more formal Mary.

Carlie brought Horace up to date on the conversation. "Mary was just telling me about the Spanish Flu in, what was it again? 1917 or 1918?"

"Yes, 1918."

Horace snapped his fingers and said, "My oldest brother was in Birmingham at Howard College. He got the flu and said a whole slew of 'em had it, but a Nurse Honeycutt — he never forgot her name — kept them all alive. People died all over Birmingham, but none of the Howard students did. My brother thought the world of Honeycutt."

Mary said, "Being in New York City during the flu was quite challenging for my parents. They kept me indoors as much as possible. That's all they knew to do. Even a few years later, after the danger of the pandemic had passed, they still kept me inside most of the time. Partially out of habit, and partially out of lingering fear."

Taking a sip of cold lemonade, Mary went on, "My parents were young and doing the best they could to make their way in the city, but they eventually realized how lonely I was. Our apartment building was full of girls who were much older and too busy to play with me, or little boys who were quite disgusting, so I entertained myself most days."

"I grew up with brothers," Carlie laughed, "so you don't have to tell me about gross little boys."

"Playing alone builds imagination," Horace said. "I had 10 brothers and sisters, and never once had to think of anything to do. I just woke up, and there was always something going on." He lowered his voice. "Serving as a pastor all those years later, I loved my large, vocal congregations, but I always cherished the quiet time of writing my sermons. Ahh, peace and quiet." He closed his eyes at the memory.

Mary said, "My father had a quiet job in the center of the most chaotic place in the world. He was an engineer with the Port of New York. When he returned home every evening, I always asked him to tell me about the ships and people he'd seen."

She blotted the perspiring glass with a napkin and said, "My mother tried to keep me busy by turning me into a little homemaker. By the time I was 4 years old, I could boil an egg, darn socks, and hem the edge of a handkerchief."

Horace's eyes twinkled as he shouted, "Good! I have some socks you can mend!"

As she rolled her eyes upward, Mary let out a "Humph!" and said, "Go darn your own smelly socks."

Carlie laughed and pretended to scold them. "Okay, you two, be nice."

It was then that Annie emerged from her cottage and joined the others on the porch. "Hello, old girl!" Horace called.

"Watch it, buster," Annie sweetly sang as she gave a gentle swat to the back of his head.

"Do you remember the Spanish Flu in 1918?" Carlie asked Annie. "Mary's telling us what she remembers from The Big Apple."

"Actually, I wasn't born until 1920, so I missed it,"Annie said as she eased herself down onto the metal glider facing the rocking chairs. "But I heard all about it years later from my uncles who traveled the world in the military. It was devastating. I don't think we'll ever see anything like it again."

Carlie poured lemonade for Annie and said, "Mary, tell us more about your parents."

"Well, in addition to his regular job at the Port, my father, who was named Joseph, was also a member of a jazz band. They played every now and then at the neighborhood club. He played both the saxophone and piano, and when he'd practice in our apartment, the neighbors across the hallway would cheer. I remember dancing around the room while he played. He said I was his little flapper."

"Oh, the flappers!" shouted Horace. "We heard about those dangerous big-city women."

The small group laughed and waited while Mary gathered her thoughts.

"Knowing how lonely I was and seeing how much I loved the neighbor's new baby, my parents decided to get me a baby doll for Christmas. They thought I would stay busy playing house. Mother, whose name was Margaret, gave Father explicit instructions on the type of doll to buy. The very next day, which was only a week before Christmas, he left work early, and walked through snow flurries to get to Schwarz Toy Bazaar so he could find the doll."

"Schwarz? I've heard of FAO Schwarz," Carlie said.

"Yes, it's the same company, but when I was a little girl, it was called Schwarz Toy Bazaar. Even back then, they had all the best toys. Schwarz's was a magical place."

Mary felt uneasy being new to the group, but she continued, "Over the years, my father loved telling me the story of how he walked into the store, intent on getting the baby doll Mother had described, but stopped in his tracks when he saw something that immediately changed his mind. Father decided right then and there to alter the plan."

Becoming a bit nervous about sharing so much with people who were practically strangers, Mary cleared her throat, determined to bring the story to a quick end.

"Not worried at all about what Mother would think, he spent more money than planned and bought a completely different doll that looked like a little girl, not a baby as they had originally discussed. This wasn't a doll to rock or cuddle. Father said he knew in his heart that I would love this doll much better than one that looked like an infant."

Leaning forward, Annie opened her eyes wide. She asked, "Well, did you like it?"

"Oh, I loved her. She was the best Christmas present ever." Mary thought for a moment, then softly repeated, "The best Christmas ever."

Overhearing Mary's final comment, Horace looked straight into her eyes and said, "One of the great mysteries in life is how our Father knows exactly what we need, sometimes before we ever ask."

TARABELLA

Mary grows up

After surviving a lonely childhood, the years flew by for Mary. Their small family of three struggled through the Great Depression along with the rest of the country, but life moved on with celebrations, parties, Easter egg hunts, school plays, birthdays, graduations, and many more Christmases.

Mary remained an only child and Joseph and Margaret adored her.

Mary grew up and fell in love with a handsome man named Patrick, who had come to New York from Ireland.

Patrick and Mary were married in St. John the Baptist Church on West 31st Street and later had a little girl named Lenora. When Lenora grew up, she and her husband had a little boy named Robert. He was Mary's first grandson, and they nicknamed him "Bobby." I met Bobby when we were both students in college. Now, I call him "Bob," and I also call him my husband. We were married in 1993.

By the time Bob and I were married, Mary had grown into a grandmother and lived alone. As my new grandmother-in-law, she said I could call her "Mimi." I loved hearing Mimi's stories about her life in long-ago New York City. Everything seemed so different from my life in a small Southern town. I often asked her to tell me about her school or where she went shopping. Mimi always had great stories about formal dances, crowded museums, and fancy dresses. She sounded like a fun teenager, full of life.

I listened to her every detail as she told me about attending the very first Macy's Thanksgiving Day Parade with her friend

Kathleen and how they laughed at nursery rhyme characters marching past. She recalled how she and Kathleen played on the sunny rooftop of their apartment building, where the women hung laundry to dry. The girls always seemed to meet interesting people as they strolled through the neighborhood.

I realized that even though Mimi had been an only child, she ended up having a close friend and many wonderful adventures in the most amazing city in the world.

TARABELLA

What did you say?

Although our regional and generational differences in speech made it tricky at times to understand one another, I was mesmerized with the details Mimi remembered of places she'd gone and things she'd seen. The way she wove stories was captivating. A blend of an old Knickerbocker accent and an Irish brogue with a hint of something totally unfamiliar, it was unlike any other accent I'd ever heard. I also loved her vocabulary that sprinkled old-fashioned words into every conversation. If she liked something, she'd say it was the "bee's knees" or "the berries." But almost daily, my Southern accent completely baffled her.

Mimi once thought I was talking about a "ball," when in fact, I was asking if she'd like some "boiled peanuts." "Ballwhat-nuts?" she asked. "No, b-oil-ed," I had to repeat. Whether she understood me or not, she politely declined the Southern delicacy. Mimi's accent sounded like Katharine Hepburn's and made her stories sound elegant. She made me laugh every time she used the words "hooligan" and "tommyrot."

It occurred to me that Mimi may have kept in touch with her friend Kathleen. After all these years, wouldn't it be fun to meet Mimi's childhood friend? The next time I saw Mimi, I asked if Kathleen still lived in New York, but Mimi's face clouded as she looked down at her wrinkled hands. She sighed and said Kathleen wasn't a real girl.

Kathleen was a doll.

"A doll?"

I was beyond confused. Maybe it was due to our drawls and accents. Was a "doll" an old-timey thing to call your friend? Mimi had spoken so matter-of-factly about her friendship with Kathleen, I just knew she must be real. Details of each story wove the tale of a very real friend, not a toy.

Mimi's voice slipped into the tone used when offering condolences. She explained that finding Kathleen beneath the Christmas tree when she was four and a half years old was the happiest moment of her childhood. "She was perfect. Absolutely perfect for me."

For such a joyful memory, her voice sounded flat.

Mimi paused, then continued, "It was popular in those days to take your doll with you to social events. All the girls would meet in the park, pushing our dolls in prams. My mother made us matching dresses, and people would rave about how darling we looked."

As Mimi sat quietly for a moment, I thought of my own childhood dolls, who were carefully packed away in a closet where they could have a "little rest." I thought how much fun it would be to pull Kathleen out of storage and see this doll myself. She must be something amazing.

"Do you think I could see Kathleen?"

Mimi's voice dropped even lower as she explained she no longer had Kathleen.
"My parents and I attended Mass one Sunday morning, and I left Kathleen at home, sitting in the living room. When we returned, we saw the neighbors running in and out of our apartment."

"What were they doing?" I asked.

"They were putting out a fire."

The old furnace that heated the apartment had exploded, which was a common danger in those days, and everything in the room had been destroyed — including Kathleen.

"I often brought her to church with me, but that day, I left her at home." Tears ran down Mimi's soft cheeks.

"I just wanted her to be warm."

I could barely breathe and didn't know what to say. Little Mary's heartache had lasted eight decades and remained heavy even now that she had grown into our "Mimi."

Our darling grandmother had carried real grief and real guilt for a real friend.
That kind of love indeed made Kathleen a real girl.

TARABELLA

A fussy baby

B ob rushed me to the hospital to have our second baby. After we held our new son in our arms, Bob rushed home to check on our 3-year-old, who was staying with his uncle. "Back in two hours," Bob promised.

While we were left alone, the newborn and I couldn't get comfortable. He fussed and cried, and I was exhausted. This hospital didn't have a nursery because they believed it was best for the baby to stay in the room with their mother. Obviously, the person who made that decision had never given birth.

Just when I thought I was going to burst into tears from exhaustion, Mimi walked into the hospital room. She had come to see our new baby and was thrilled to learn he had just been born.

She held out her arms and said, "Let me hold him."

"His name is Joseph, like your daddy," I told her.

Upon hearing this news, Mimi's face looked like it had been splashed with a cold mixture of joy and surprise. She broke into a big smile, then sat next to my bed and rocked our little Joseph, who immediately fell into a peaceful sleep . . . as did I.

After a few days, Mimi returned home and said she missed us. We missed her too

It's more than a thingamabob

We soon realized it was time for Mimi to be near family who loved her. She was growing older and loved playing with our boys, so we asked if she would like to join us in Alabama.

She feigned shock and said, "Me? In Alabama?"

"Yes, you'll love it," we assured her.

"Do they even have grocery stores in Al-a-bama?" Mimi asked with a hint of snippiness.

"Yes, and the people read and write as well," I teased.

"You're full of beans," she laughed. Mimi was truly grateful to be joining us in coastal Alabama, even if she thought it was the end of the earth.

We found a two-bedroom cottage for her in a senior living community near our home. With a small kitchen and living room, it shared a large porch with other cottages that overlooked a meadow full of rabbits, and suited her perfectly.

On moving day, Bob arranged Mimi's furniture while I helped unpack the stack of boxes. When we were nearly finished, I opened an old trunk full of crocheted doilies and tablecloths. Beneath the linens I found a raggedy-looking box. The corners were crushed, but something about it intrigued me.

"What's in here?" I asked, as Mimi whisked past the doorway carrying a few books.

"Probably full of thingamabobs," she laughed.

"Ooo, I love thingamabobs," I thought, as I gave the box a gentle shake. With great caution, I lifted the lid, which almost fell apart in my hand. What I found inside was in even worse shape than the rotted box.

There was a strange odor. "What in the world?" I thought. I wasn't sure what I was looking at. It was dirty and appeared to be pieces of pottery. Was it a broken vase or a smashed bowl of some kind? Whatever it was, why would it be covered in dirt, and why would Mimi save it all these years?

As I used my finger to poke one of the pieces aside, I saw a tiny — hand.

"Eew! What is this?" The musty, smoky smell was stronger now.

Mimi kept bustling around, arranging cups and saucers in her new kitchen cupboard as I sat in the next room with this strange discovery.

I kept sifting through the dirt, then saw another miniature arm with fingers, and finally at the bottom of the box was a dirty face staring back at me.

My eyes must have been the size of golf balls.

This box held pieces of a doll. A doll covered in black soot!

"Oh, there's no way in tarnation . . ." I said.

I called out, "Hey, Mimi! Look what I found!"

She breezed past the doorway but didn't even stop to look as I asked, "Is this Kathleen?"

I guess because she was overwhelmed with relocating and tired from the day's work, she dismissed me with a wave of her hand and flatly said, "No." She didn't even come close to where I was sitting to see for herself. Maybe she thought I was looking at an old photo, or maybe she didn't even hear me correctly, but she acted as if I had hurt her feelings by even mentioning Kathleen's name. She walked away and made it clear she didn't want to be bothered with anything other than organizing her kitchen.

I felt like I had been scolded. Mimi's response was so brusque, I realized the subject of Kathleen was not to be discussed — ever.

So, I took the box home.

TARABELLA

Don't talk to strangers

There was indeed a learning curve for the senior New Yorker as she attempted to adapt to her new Southern home. Mimi was amazed to see how beautiful our city was and loved living close enough to visit her two great-grandsons several times a week.

When she'd come to our house for dinner, I always tried to use a white tablecloth, because she claimed it made everything taste better.

I admired Mimi's embroidered handkerchiefs, and she gave me a few to carry. "They really do make sense," I told her.

She admired my collection of deviled egg plates. "They really do make sense," she said.

While standing in line at the post office one day, she asked, "Do you know everyone in town?"

Someone had just greeted me by saying, "It's a beautiful day, isn't it?" I smiled and responded, "Yes, I think the pollen has eased off a bit."

"No, everyone here talks to each other," I explained. "We're just being friendly."

"You shouldn't talk to strangers," she whispered with great seriousness as she clutched her purse to her chest.

"How else would I ever get gardening tips or learn Mr. Gene lost his dog?" I laughed and reassured her, "It's good to talk to strangers. That's how we turn them into friends."

Poor Mimi was in culture shock.

When a kindhearted neighbor left a small box of homegrown vegetables on Mimi's doorstep, she was horrified that someone thought she needed charity.

"Who would leave these vegetables here? There's no telling where in the world they came from. Do I look like I'm starving?" she demanded.

I explained it was our custom to share the bounty of our backyard gardens with friends and neighbors.

"But there's no note," she complained.

"They'll probably mention it the next time they see you. They'll say, 'How did you like the squash and tomatoes I left you last week?' You can't tell them you threw them out."

Just as she was catching on and starting to understand the ways of her new hometown, I warned Mimi about zucchini season. "We're overrun with so much zucchini around here, people can't get rid of it. It's the only time of the year we lock our cars, for fear someone will toss a bag of zucchini in the backseat while we're not looking. It piles up like Southern snow. If enough people leave it on your porch, you may get barricaded in your own house."

By this time, Mimi knew not to take me seriously, but just to be on the safe side, peeked out her window a few times a day to keep an eye out for "those vegetable people."

I came home one day and told Bob, "I think Mimi has finally settled in and understands that all these people talking to her are just trying to be nice and welcome her. She's going to love Alabama after all."

Bob looked over the top of his computer and said, "Whether she ever admits it or not."

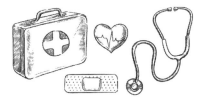

A flower-covered bungalow

Spreading the grungy porcelain doll parts on a newspaper in my kitchen, I was convinced I had discovered the battered, bruised, and burned Kathleen. But there were so many questions. Could Mimi's mother, Margaret, have boxed up the pieces of the doll thinking she'd have her repaired, but then lost track of the box? Or perhaps this wasn't Kathleen at all. What if this was another doll someone had given Mimi, or even something she purchased at a thrift sale?

Who was I kidding? Mimi didn't go to thrift sales.

Maybe these doll pieces didn't even belong to the same doll but had been intended for a spooky Halloween display of some sort. They certainly looked gruesome enough to scare a little trick-or-treater. There's no way this pile of soot-covered junk was ever a beloved doll.

Mimi was dismayed our small town didn't have a grand theatre or a large department store like New York. But we did have a pecan-shelling plant, cotton fields, a Piggly Wiggly, and of all things . . . a flower-covered bungalow with a sign that read "Doll Hospital."

I'd never even noticed it before, but as I drove down Morphy Avenue one day, a glimmer of sun bounced off the sign. I was so excited that I almost ran off the road. I drove home as fast as possible and grabbed the dingy box, then turned around and raced back downtown.

Holding baby Joseph on my hip and the box of scorched doll parts in my other hand, we entered the quaint hospital and

were amazed to see a flurry of activity —
like a real hospital.

As I handed over the beat-up box to the
doll doctors, I told them, "If you had an
emergency entrance, I would have used it."

"I swanee! I think you need the burn
unit," one of them said when she lifted the
lid.

As I watched the women examine the
contents, I felt anxious, as if awaiting a real
diagnosis that could bring bad news. What
if they told me there was no hope? What if
they told me, "No, these pieces and parts
belong to a doll from the 1970s"? The
possibility of disappointment was ominous,
and I prepared myself to be crushed by
their analysis.

The experts went to work, brushing and
wiping, and at one point, used tweezers and
a magnifying glass.

A sad Southern benediction over a
hopeless soul followed.

"I declare!"

"Mercy daisy!"

"What in the Sam Hill?"

And finally, "Good gravy."

I shifted Joseph to my other hip as even he looked fascinated with the medical sleuthing going on in front of us. They finally announced, "This doll was made in the 1920s."

A flutter of hope danced through my heart. Could it be?

I always want my surgeon and my pilot to be the most confident person in the room, and in the same way, the doll doctor reassured me of her total competency with her authoritative announcement, "I know exactly what kind of doll this is."

As she held the sooty bald head up to the light, she continued, "She is a Schoenau & Hoffmeister from Germany, with a porcelain bisque body that can obviously withstand a fire. I can clean her up, put her back together, and order new clothing. I'll find a wig just like the one she came with, and by the time I finish, she'll look brand new."

Then she gave a firm nod of her head and added, "Trust me, she'll feel much better than she does now."

"Yes!" I felt hope sprinkled with excitement — one of my favorite emotions — like when your football team makes a fourth-quarter interception.

I bounced Joseph in the air, and he mirrored my joy with a drooly toothless giggle. It was a good thing he wasn't talking yet, or he would have surely told Mimi what I was doing. I was still unsure what she'd think. The possible outcomes made me nervous. This could either be an amazing victory or a dismal failure. What was I thinking?

TARABELLA

Coming home

A few weeks later, the hospital called to say my doll was ready to be discharged. I was excited but didn't know what to expect. I envisioned a doll like the ones I had played with, which were babies small enough to cuddle. Even though Mimi had told me all about her adventures with Kathleen, the only description she'd ever offered was that she had brown hair and a sweet face.

The doctors at the hospital gathered 'round to see my expression when I saw this repaired, resurrected, and reconstructed doll for the first time.

What I saw in their arms was nothing like I had expected. This wasn't a baby doll, but instead looked like a little girl. At 26 inches tall, she had brunette ringlets that bounced on her shoulders and sparkling brown eyes that made it seem as if she was really looking around the room. I seriously stopped breathing when she looked right at me.

The doll's face had a peaceful look, and her mouth was parted just enough for tiny teeth to show, making it seem as if she was in the middle of sharing a secret. I took her in my arms and felt the huggable body almost cling to me like a real child's, yet her arms and legs were heavy bisque, so she was able to sit alone. No longer smelling of ashes, she somehow had the scent of roses and Juicy Fruit. Just like a grandmother.

I was completely charmed.

But was this Kathleen?

Only Mimi would know for sure.

Did we do the right thing?

Christmas 2000 was a month away. It had been exactly 80 years since my husband's great-grandfather, Joseph, had given his 4-year-old daughter a doll. Should we attempt to recreate that Christmas? It was risky because we still weren't 100% certain this doll was really the one and only Kathleen.

"You know how practical she is," Bob thought aloud.

"Picky is more like it," I said, even though we both knew I kind of liked Mimi's pickiness. It gave her an air of distinction and wasn't intimidating at all; rather, it made her more of a lovable character. Many of my New York grandmother-in-law's mannerisms reflected my own Southern manners. We saw eye to eye on more things than we had ever imagined. Yet when it came to this doll, I wasn't sure what to expect. I didn't want to dredge up hurtful memories.

"If this isn't Kathleen, she's going to think we're weird for giving her a random doll," Bob said. "Do you think she'd even be insulted?"

"I don't know. Every grandmother still has the heart of a little girl inside her, and I know the little Mary inside of Mimi would give anything to see Kathleen again. It's a chance we've got to take."

I thought some more, then added, "Besides, if this isn't Kathleen, then why would someone have bothered boxing up burnt doll parts to save all these years?"

Bob said, "Too bad we don't know what Kathleen really looked like so we could confirm everything." He was troubled with the plan.

As December spun by with parties, church events, and decorating, my endearing optimism finally won Bob over, and he reluctantly agreed to help me wrap the doll in a large gift box.

As we taped up one side, he said, "You know, Mimi loves being with us, but she still hasn't made many friends her own age."

It was true. She was happy, yet lonely. Her retirement neighborhood was full of people who had grown up together in Alabama, and she felt like an outsider. Not since she'd been a little girl in New York had she been without friends.

We snuggled the doll down in a nest of tissue paper, and Bob said, "I hope this doll doesn't embarrass her." I tossed the big red bow I'd made at his head and said, "Way to be positive." But Bob was touching on what I was afraid to say. Who wants to hurt their grandmother's feelings? Especially at Christmas.

Worrying about the unknown can make you second-guess everything. But playing it safe rarely ends in magic.

The moment of truth

Alabama Gulf Coast Christmases can be chilly or tropical, and it would be a miracle if we ever had snow, so it was no surprise when we awoke on December 25th to "festive humidity" that made the candy canes stick together. We attempted the Southern trick of lowering the thermostat while lighting a fire in the rarely used fireplace to provide at least a few moments of "winter wonderland."

My large extended family descended upon our house, with my grandparents, parents, aunts, uncles, and cousins all bringing side dishes to accompany the turkey. Our meal resembled a church dinner on the grounds, with a little bit of everything shuttled in casserole dishes and bowls covered with tea towels and aluminum foil. The aroma was amazing as lids were lifted from cheesy casseroles with crunchy toppings, bowls of homegrown vegetables, pans of dressing (never stuffing), and relish trays with pickled okra grown by my granddaddy. Multiple plates of deviled eggs sprinkled with paprika sat next to the basket of biscuits and cornbread with a crock of soft butter beside.

We unfolded the gate leg table specifically for desserts. Cookies shaped like reindeer, bells, and snowmen were joined by chocolate pie, coconut cake, pound cake, lemon squares, and of course, a Jell-O mold, which in Alabama, depending upon the shape and fruit content, could be considered a salad. Mimi was appreciative we used the Lenox Holiday china atop a Christmas tablecloth. I wouldn't have had it any other way.

Everyone settled down while my grandfather opened the family Bible, just as his father had done, and read aloud the story from Luke. We listened to the same words we'd heard our entire lives on December 25th about God's gift to us in Bethlehem.

"Fear not: for behold, I bring you good tidings of great joy, which shall be to all people. For unto you is born this day in the city of David a Savior, which is Christ the Lord."

We closed with a prayer, during which my older son decided he could stand it no longer and took the opportunity to scoot closer to the pile of presents. When we said, "Amen," chaos erupted with boxes, paper, bows, and laughter swirling through the room.

Ironically, Dean Martin's version of "Let It Snow" played in the background of our balmy festivities. The adults were as animated as the children, yet Mimi sat poised and calm, taking in the revelry of her new big Southern family. We waited for a few moments as Mimi first unwrapped a box of her favorite candy, then a new picture frame.

The music played, "But if you really hold me tight, all the way home I'll be warm."

Someone called out over the music, "Who's this big present for?" The time of truth had finally arrived.

"The tag says, 'To Mimi'!"

Mimi's eyes grew wide. "For me? Why, I can't imagine."

Bob placed the gift in front of her, and as those who lived through the Great Depression are known to do, the resourceful woman took her time to carefully preserve the bows and ribbons, then smoothed the paper to reuse another day. We were fidgety and unsure of what the next minute would bring. Bob and I shot looks of concern at one other as we scanned her face.

"Just open it! Open it! Open it!" I wanted to shout.

The box was finally opened, and within a split second, Mimi caught her breath and whispered, "Kathleen!"

She didn't even need to lift the doll from the box before she was in tears and saying her name over and over. "Kathleen, oh, Kathleen!"

It really and truly was the one and only Kathleen, home at last with her Mary.

The beaming face we saw at that moment wasn't our old Mimi but was instead the tender face of little Mary.

I could clearly see the 4-year-old in her New York apartment, clutching Kathleen to her chest and spinning round and round in front of the Christmas tree while Margaret and Joseph held one another. The image was so vivid, I had to squeeze my eyes to refocus on the Christmas at hand, and as I did, I sniffed back tears of my own.

Kathleen had returned to her friend. Tears streamed down Mimi's face as she hugged the doll. It was as if the two had been transported back to Christmas morning, 1920

Love lasts longer

Mimi took Kathleen to her cottage, and from that day forward, Kathleen would be in a new place each time we visited: one day displayed on a chair in the living room, the next day on the sofa. Sometimes Kathleen would be taking a nap on the bed.

Kathleen accompanied Mimi outdoors to visit neighbors, especially the ones who were kind enough to share their vegetables. The long-lost friend connected Mimi to new friends who had been wanting to get to know her better. Everyone wanted to know where the doll had come from, and Mimi was more than happy to share the story with them.

Talking to complete strangers became normal for the newcomer. "I have a doll with hair just like yours," she told a curly-headed little girl who was standing with her mother at the coffee shop. "Her name is Kathleen. What's your name?"

Kathleen didn't just sit in the corner like a decoration or prop. She was a childhood friend who had returned home.

Once comforting a lonely little girl in a big city, she now comforted a lonely great-grandmother in an unfamiliar small town. The two of them had eight decades of stories to share, although I'm sure Mimi's stories were much better than Kathleen's.

"I traveled on a cruise ship."

"I was stuck in a box."

"I worked in a doctor's office."

"I was stuck in a box."

"I missed you."

"I missed you too."

And then the smiling mouth, ready to share a secret, must have added, "I always knew you'd find me again."

Kathleen listened to all of Mimi's tales of a life well lived, of heartaches, achievements, and celebrations. She was the same loving friend from long ago, and the two reminisced about their happy days together.

One Saturday, Bob took the boys to Julwin's for their traditional Saturday breakfast, which gave me a morning alone. I decided to visit Mimi, and she invited me to sit with her in the living room. We drank coffee from hand-painted china cups and nibbled on cookies. As we talked about hurricane season and her new neighbors, the conversation turned to her childhood days in New York. Kathleen sat next to her on the sofa and looked as if she was participating in the story.

Mimi looked over at her old friend and said, "I'm sure my father never dreamed I'd still have Kathleen by my side at this age." Then she laughed and said, "But neither did I." After a minute of gazing out on the meadow, she said, "I guess love lasts longer than we do."

A familiar face

We were heartbroken when Mimi died. Joseph was old enough to know his Mimi was no longer with us, and he and his brother cried for days.

As I was packing away Mimi's things, in the same room where I had first discovered Kathleen in sooty pieces, I came across an envelope of old photographs. Flipping through a few, I saw people I'd never met, but suddenly stopped when I saw a familiar face. Among the faded images of relatives who long ago immigrated from Ireland was a black-and-white picture, of a darling little girl with a big hair bow, standing on a rooftop with her friend. There was no mistaking the friend, with dark ringlets hanging to her shoulders and a smiling mouth, ready to share a secret.

Beneath the image, someone had written, "Mary and Kathleen."

I would have recognized them anywhere.

The End.

TARABELLA

Epilogue

I hope your favorite childhood toy is still with you, whether it's in your arms, or in your heart.

    Kathleen lives at my house now, and someday, when my son Joseph has a little girl, I think Kathleen would like to go live with her. This yet-to-be-born baby girl would be Mary's great-great-granddaughter.

"What happens if Joseph doesn't have a little girl?" you may wonder. Well, I think toys that were truly loved will always find their way into the arms of another good-hearted child.

"Kathleen is an antique now. Would you really allow another child to play with her?"

is another question often asked. I say, "Yes. This doll is too full of love to be kept on a shelf. She needs another child to love her, and besides, if she can withstand a fire and 80 years of confinement to a box, she can withstand another 4-year-old little girl."

Until then, Kathleen and I enjoy our time together at my house. She's always thanking me for taking her to the hospital. I give her a wink and thank her for loving Mimi as she grew older.